W9-ABB-883

Holiday Makers

CRAFTS FOR

HALLOWEEN

Ben Macgregor

PowerKiDS
press.

New York

Published in 2023 by The Rosen Publishing Group, Inc.
29 East 21st Street, New York, NY 10010

Written by Ben Macgregor

Designed by Alix Wood

Projects devised by Ben Macgregor

All photographs © Alix Wood Books

Cataloging-in-Publication Data

Names: Macgregor, Ben.
Title: Crafts for Halloween / Ben Macgregor.
Description: New York : Powerkids Press, 2023. | Series: Holiday makers | Includes index.
Identifiers: ISBN 9781725337893 (pbk.) | ISBN 9781725337916 (library bound) | ISBN 9781725337909 (6pack) | ISBN 9781725337923 (ebook)
Subjects: LCSH: Halloween decorations--Juvenile literature. | Handicraft--Juvenile literature.
Classification: LCC TT900.H32 M33 2023 | DDC 745.594'1646--dc23

Manufactured in the United States of America

CPSIA Compliance Information: Batch #CSPK23. For further information contact Rosen Publishing, New York, New York at 1-800-237-9932.

Find us on 🅕 📷

Contents

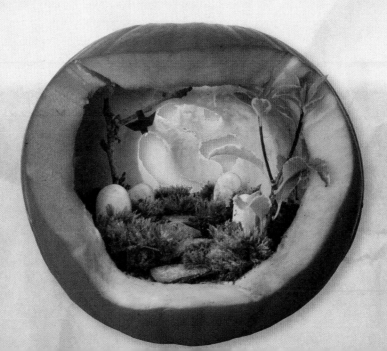

Get Holiday Making!

Make your home look super spooky with these fun crafts for Halloween. You can make decorations, some trick-or-treat goodies to eat, and even a bag to put them in!

What will you need?

The projects use fairly standard crafting supplies, such as card stock, yarn, duct tape, PVA glue, pencil and paper, markers, tape, a hole punch, and some pipe cleaners. Scissors, string, and a glue stick are needed too.

BEWARE! Acrylic paint and PVA glue will stain once it has dried. Cover yourself and all your surfaces before you paint. If it gets on your clothes, wash it off right away.

No Black Card Stock?

No problem, use purple or navy blue instead. They look just as dark and spooky.

Pumpkin-Carving Tips and Tricks

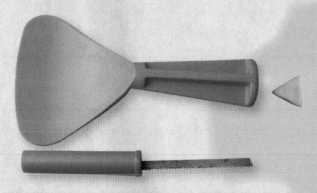

If you can, use a pumpkin-carving kit. The little saw is safer than a knife, and the scoop really helps get the gunk out. Otherwise, use a spoon, and ask an adult to help find a suitable, safe knife.

Cut the top off your pumpkin at an angle. This keeps the lid from falling into the pumpkin. If you cut it straight up and down, it'll fall in!

Paint Mixing

You can mix all the colors you need with just red, blue, yellow, and white paint!

Orange - Mix a little red into some yellow.

Green - Mix a little blue into some yellow.

Brown - Mix red and yellow. Add a little blue.

Pink - Add a little red to some white.

Black - Mix blue, red, and a little yellow.

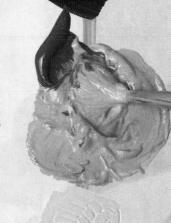

Pumpkin Carving

Halloween just isn't Halloween without a pumpkin. Try this trick to transfer your design onto the pumpkin. It makes cutting the shapes a lot easier.

You will need...

- a pumpkin
- a pumpkin cutter and scoop
- paper and pencil
- round object
- skewer

1

Adult help needed

See page 5 for how to cut the top off the pumpkin. You may want an adult to help you. Scoop out the seeds.

2

Find a round object that is smaller than your pumpkin.

3

Draw around the object.

Then draw your design in the circle.

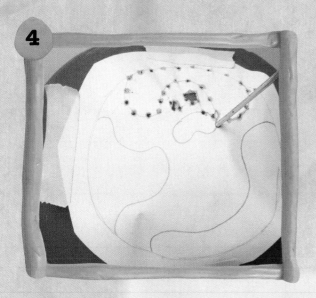 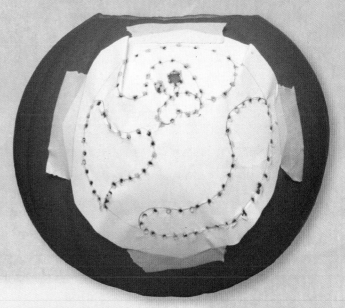

4

Tape your design to the pumpkin. Pierce holes all around the drawing using a skewer.

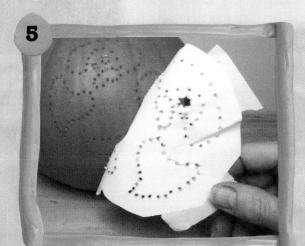

5

Peel away the paper to reveal your outline.

6

Join the dots! Use a pumpkin cutter to carve out the design.

Ghoulish Jars

These candleholder jars look great on your doorstep or fireplace. You can paint them in all kinds of different ways.

1

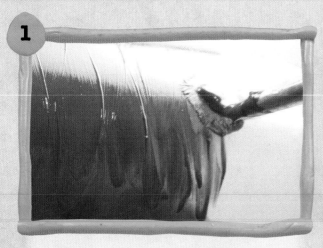

Cover a jar using orange acrylic paint. You can mix yellow and red to make orange.

2

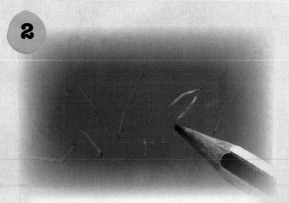

Scratch your pumpkin design into the paint using a pencil.

3

Then paint your pumpkin.

You could paint ghosts using glow-in-the-dark paint!

4

Tape the end of the bandage to the jar rim. Wind the bandage around the jar. Leave a gap for the eyes. Tape the end in place.

5

Draw twice around a large coin on white card stock, and a small coin on black card stock. Cut out the circles. Glue them together as shown.

6

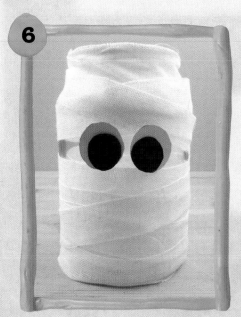

Glue or tape the eyes in place.

Candles are dangerous. Use battery candles inside your spooky jars.

Yarn Mummy

These mummies are really cute to have hanging around. If you don't have any yarn, you can use string or strips of white material instead.

1

Draw a circle at the top of a sheet of black card stock.

Then add the arms and legs.

2

Draw two eyes on white paper. Color them with black marker. Glue them onto the face.

3

Tape the end of the yarn to the back of the mummy's head. Start to wind the yarn all around the mummy.

4

5

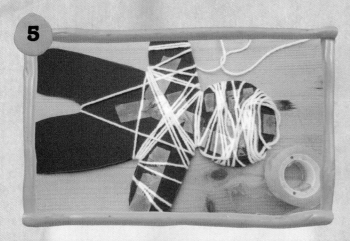

Now and then, tape the yarn at the back to keep it in place.

6

When you are happy, cut the yarn with scissors.

7

Moving the yarn away, punch a hole in the head.

8

Thread a length of yarn through the hole.

Spooky Window

Turn a few sheets of black paper into a scary window display. These windows should really spook out your neighborhood!

You will need...

- three large sheets of black paper
- scissors
- white pencil
- some white paper
- masking tape

1

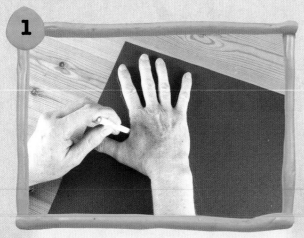

On a large sheet of black paper, trace around your hand and bent arm.

2

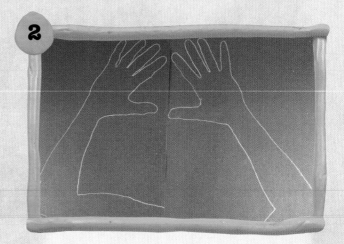

On another sheet of paper, repeat with your other arm.

3

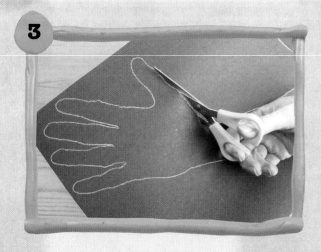

Cut out both arms using the scissors.

4

Draw a ghost on another sheet of paper.

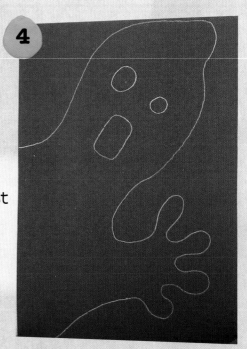

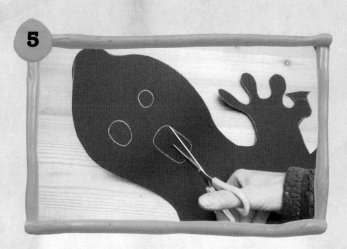

5

Pierce a hole in the center of the ghost's eyes and mouth to make cutting them out easier.

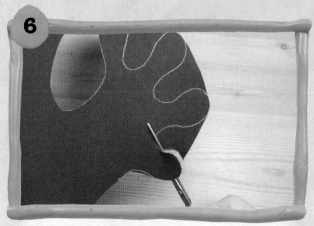

6

To cut the hand out, cut around the whole hand first, then cut around each finger.

7

Tape the silhouettes on the inside of a window. Then tape white paper to cover the window.

Trick-or-Treat Bag

These bags are even waterproof!
Duct tape likes sticking to itself,
so ask an adult to help at step 3.

You will need...

- orange and black
  duct tape
- scissors
- masking tape
- pencil

1

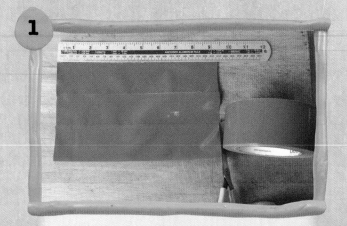

Cut a 9-inch (23 cm) strip of
tape and lightly stick it to a
board. Slightly overlap another
length along its bottom.
Repeat until you have a square.

2

Make three more duct tape
squares in the same way.
Don't worry if the edges are
a little jagged. You'll trim
them later.

3

Adult help needed

Tape one square onto the board, sticky
side up. Carefully stick another square,
sticky side down, onto it. You may want
adult help. It can be tricky!

4

Repeat with the other two sheets. Then
tape the two sides together along three
edges to make a bag.

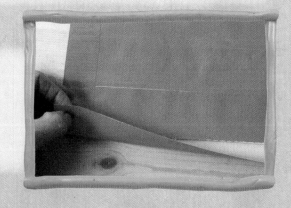

5

To make the handle, fold two long strips of tape in half. Trim off any excess.

6

Tape the handles to the inside of the bag.

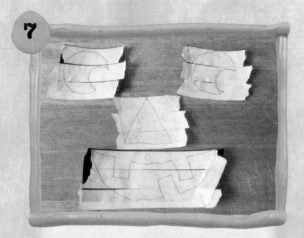

7

Stick masking tape on pieces of black tape. Draw on your pumpkin eyes, nose, and mouth.

8

Cut out, then stick on your pumpkin face. Then peel off the masking tape.

Flashlight Shadows

Project some spooky bats onto your walls this Halloween! You may want an adult to help you cut out the stencil.

You will need...

- a flashlight
- white paper
- black card stock
- scissors
- a pencil
- black tape

1

Place the flashlight on the black card stock, lens side down. Trace around the circle.

2

Cut out the circle. Place that circle on the white paper and trace around the outline.

3

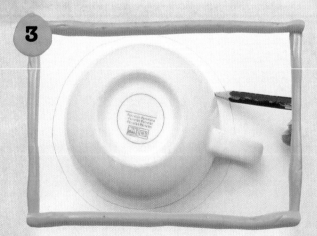

Find a smaller circular object. Center it and draw around it, so you have a donut shape.

4

Draw bats in the circle. Make sure they join the outer circle somewhere.

5

Adult help needed

6

Cut out the areas that are shaded in this picture. You may want an adult to help you.

Tape the cutout to the flashlight lens. Tape all around, so no light escapes through the gaps.

Now shine your flashlight onto a wall.

Halloween Lollipops

So easy to make, these lollipop costumes make great trick-or-treat gifts. You could poke some holes in a pumpkin and put the lollipops in the holes. Place the pumpkin on your doorstep and see if anyone dares to take one!

You will need...

- two black pipe cleaners
- two lollipops
- white paper
- two tissues
- a hole punch
- black trash bag
- black marker
- string and a glue stick
- scissors

1

Place a lollipop in the center of a tissue and wrap the tissue around it.

2

Place a second tissue over the top of the first. Wrap that tissue too.

3

Tie a length of string around the ghost's neck.

Draw on the face using a marker.

4

5

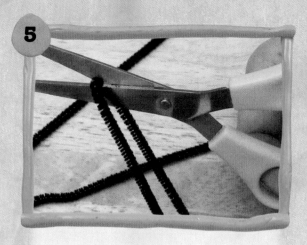

Cut two pipe cleaners in half.

6

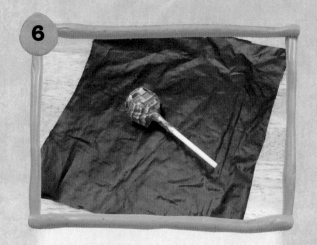

Cut a square of trash bag. Wrap it around the lollipop.

7

Twist the pipe cleaners around the stick to make the legs.

8

Make two circles using the hole punch. Color the eyes using a marker.

Glue the eyes in place using a glue stick.

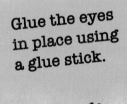

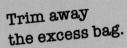

Trim away the excess bag.

Scary Rocks

It's fun to create colorful painted rocks. You can sometimes find smooth pebbles by riverbeds. Check that it's OK to take them first. You can buy them from garden nurseries, too.

You will need...

- two smooth rocks
- acrylic paint
- pencil
- paintbrush
- markers

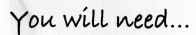

1

Paint the pebble with a coat of white paint.

2

Once the paint has dried, draw on your design.

We drew a fun Mexican Day of the Dead design.

3

Color in the details with paint.

To create the dots, use the end of the paintbrush handle.

4

5

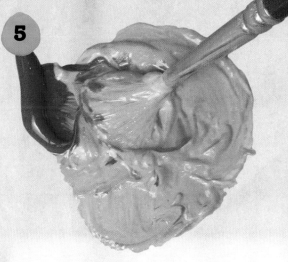

To paint the pumpkin, mix up some orange paint by adding a little red to a puddle of yellow.

6

Paint the rock orange and leave it to dry.

7

You can use markers to add the details instead.

Paint on your pumpkin face using black paint.

Maybe place your rocks on a flower pot, or on the doorstep.

Trash Bag Bat

You can hang this realistic, leathery looking bat from the ceiling and give your family a scare.

1

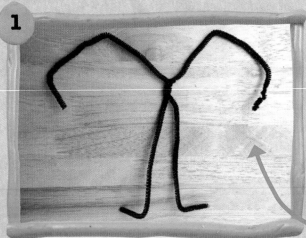

Twist two pipe cleaners together to create this shape.

2

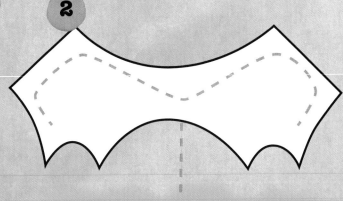

Lay your pipe cleaner shape on some white paper. Draw bat wings on the paper, a little larger than the top "M" shape.

3

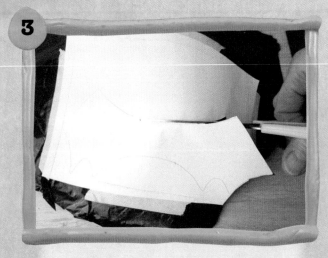

Tape the wings drawing onto a trash bag and cut around it.

4

Tape one of the black wings to the pipe cleaners as shown.

5

Tape on the second black wing to cover the pipe cleaners.

6

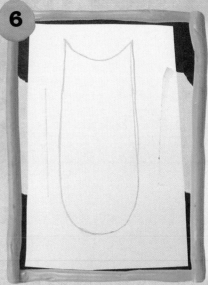

Tape some paper onto black card stock. Draw this bat body, a little taller than your wings.

7

Cut out white circles for the eyes. Stick them onto the body using a glue stick.

8

Draw on the eyes and tape the body in place.

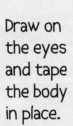

You can hang your bat by bending his pipe cleaner feet!

Spider Cookies

These cookies are yummy!
If you don't have black icing,
use thin black licorice.

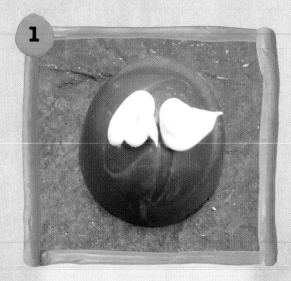

1

Pipe two white icing
blobs onto the round
chocolate.

You will need...

- plain cookies
- round chocolates
- black and white icing
  tubes
- chocolate drops

2

Place a chocolate drop
on each blob to make
the eyes.

3

To make the web, squeeze
some white icing lines across
the cookie.

4

Pipe a circle of white icing around your lines.

Place your spider body in his web.

5

6

Finally, pipe eight legs onto your spider using the black icing.

You can pipe a little smile onto your spiders, too!

Witch's Broomstick

Prop it by your door, or use it as part of a costume. This broomstick is so cheap and easy to make. Wear eye protection when you cut your twigs, in case pieces fly around.

You will need...

- a bunch of long twigs
- a larger stick
- strong rubber bands
- string
- scissors

1

Gather a big bunch of twigs. Cut them to the same length.

2

Wrap rubber bands around one end of a larger stick.

3

Poke the twigs one by one through the rubber band.

4

Gradually add more twigs to your broomstick.

5

Tightly tie one end of the string around your rubber bands.

6

Wrap the string around a few times, then tie it tightly.

Scary Fairy Garden

Make a scary fairy garden inside a hollowed-out pumpkin. You can decorate it any way you like – just make sure it's scary!

You will need...

- a pumpkin
- pumpkin carving tools
- some compost
- stones, moss, and twigs
- card stock and scissors

1

Carve a hole out of the front of a pumpkin. We reused our pumpkin from page 6-7, but you can use a plain pumpkin.

2

Put some compost in the bottom of the pumpkin.

3

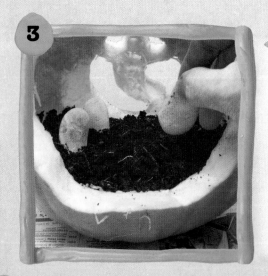

Poke stones into the compost to look like graves.

Add a little path using gravel or stones.

4

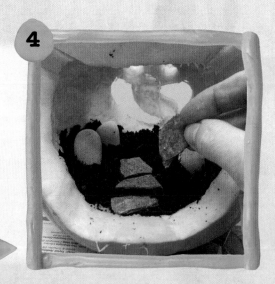

5

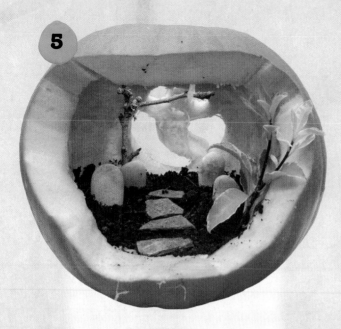

Find some twigs that look like trees.

6

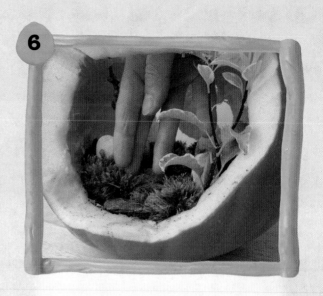

You can add a little moss or grass on top of the compost.

Maybe cut out a tiny bat to hang from one of your trees. Just fold over his feet to make him hang.

Pumpkin Garland

These squishy pumpkins are so easy to make. String them together to make some pumpkin bunting, or just dot them around the house.

You will need...

- orange yarn
- a green pipe cleaner
- scissors
- buttons
- PVA glue

1

Wrap the orange yarn around your fingers.

2

Keep wrapping until the yarn is quite thick. It needs to be enough to form a ball.

3

Slide the yarn from your hand. Make sure it stays in a ball. Cut a length of yarn, and tie it around the middle of the ball.

4

Cut a 4-inch (10 cm) length of green pipe cleaner.

5

Thread the pipe cleaner through the piece of yarn you tied around the middle of the pumpkin.

6

Twist the two pieces of pipe cleaner all the way up to make the stalk.

You could glue some button eyes onto your pumpkins.

Index